Coconut
Seed or Fruit?

By Rosie McCormick

CELEBRATION PRESS

Pearson Learning Group

Contents

Coconuts

Coconuts are usually dark brown, rough, and hairy on the outside. The outside is very hard. On the inside, they have white meat that you can eat. The meat is crunchy and sweet.

Coconuts grow on coconut palm trees. The coconut palm is a very useful tree. Every part of the tree has value for people.

Where Coconut Palms Grow

Coconut palms grow in many hot, sunny places around the world. They grow on islands and by the ocean. Many of the trees grow wild. Some are grown on large tree farms called plantations.

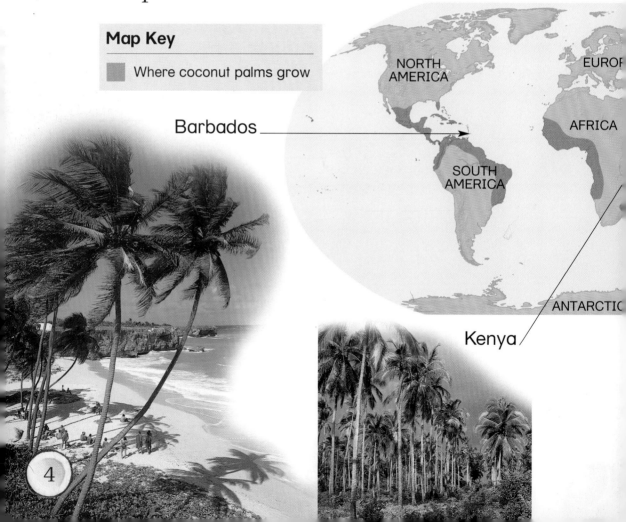

Map Key

Where coconut palms grow

NORTH AMERICA

EUROP

Barbados

AFRICA

SOUTH AMERICA

ANTARCTIC

Kenya

Sometimes coconuts fall into water. They will float. If the coconuts are washed up onto a new shore, they often sprout and grow into trees.

Coconuts float.

ASIA

AUSTRALIA

Fiji

N
W · E
S

How Coconut Palms Grow

Coconut palm trees are tall and thin. Some grow as high as a ten-story building. Their trunks are strong, but they bend with the wind. This helps keep the trees from blowing over in strong winds.

Coconut palms grow in sandy soil.
Their roots spread far out around the tree
to gather water. The many roots also hold
the trees firmly in the ground. These trees
grow new fruits year-round.
The trees may live to be
one hundred years old.

adult palm tree

leaves

coconut

leaves

coconut

young palm tree

trunk

Large green drupes grow on the coconut tree. A drupe is a fruit that usually contains one seed inside. Coconut meat grows inside the seed. It takes about a year for a coconut drupe to grow.

drupe

coconut seed
inside drupe

coconut meat
inside seed

When coconut drupes are ripe, people harvest them. Sometimes people climb the trees to cut the fruit down. Sometimes they use a long pole with a knife on one end.

The coconuts we see at the market
are really the seeds of the coconut palm trees.
A coconut is one of the largest seeds in
the world. So is a coconut a seed or a fruit?
It is both.

Uses for Coconut Palms

There is a use for every part of the coconut palm tree. The meat in the seed is good to eat. Young coconuts have a liquid inside that people can drink.

coconut milk

fresh coconut meat

dried coconut meat

Coconut meat can be dried so that it lasts a long time. The dried coconut meat is called copra. People eat copra or use it to make many things.

Coconut meat can be used to make coconut oil and coconut milk. Both of these can be used for cooking. Coconut milk is used in many recipes. The oil is used to make soap, shampoo, margarine, and candles.

coconut milk

shampoo

soap

The outer shell of a coconut is called the husk. When the coconut is young, the husk is green and smooth. Later the husk dries and turns brown. The tough, stringy fibers of the brown husk may be used to make baskets, brooms, and mats.

coconut husk
with stringy fibers

This woman is making a mat from coconut fibers.

Palm leaves are used to make roofs and walls on some buildings.

Coconut palm leaves are useful, too. In some warm climates, they are used to make roofs. The leaves can also be woven into screens, mats, and clothes.

People also use the roots and the trunk of the coconut palm. The trunks of the trees can be used to build homes and to make furniture.

Since all parts of the coconut palm can be used, it is a valuable tree. The coconut palm has provided people with food, liquid, and shelter for many, many years. In some parts of the world, this tree is an important part of life.

Index